THE
FORGOTTEN
WORLD
OF
ULOC

by Bryan Buchan

Cover and Illustrations: Kathryn Cole

SCHOLASTIC-TAB PUBLICATIONS LTD.
123 Newkirk Road, Richmond Hill, Ontario.

Copyright© 1970 by Scholastic-TAB Publications Ltd. All rights reserved.
Published by Scholastic-TAB Publications Ltd. • 123 Newkirk Road • Richmond Hill • Ontario

1st printing 1970
2nd printing 1973
3rd printing revised 1978
Printed in Canada

CONTENTS

		PAGE
1.	AT THE POND	5
2.	ULOC	11
3.	NEW PROBLEMS FOR DOUG	18
4.	PAUL CONVINCED	25
5.	HELP SNEAKS IN	31
6.	THE TRADE	38
7.	THE UNINVITED GUEST	44
8.	THE TRIP	51
9.	TWO IN A TRAP	56
10.	IN THE REALM OF SATIKA	62
11.	THE WALL BREAKS	68
12.	THE END, THE BEGINNING	76

CHAPTER ONE
AT THE POND

"Come on, Doug! It's almost time for supper!" Paul was eager to get home.

"Let's just catch the frog first," called Doug. "Then we can run home. We'll still be on time."

"I'm going now. You can run and catch up. What do you want that silly frog for anyway? You know your mother won't let you keep it." And Paul was away.

Doug rocked unsteadily back and forth on a rotting log, partly sunk in the ooze. The leopard frog had puffed itself up and floated lazily on the surface among some tangled reeds, just beyond Doug's reach.

"How can you live in this water?" wondered the boy aloud. "It sure smells terrible. Come a little nearer, so I can grab you."

The frog slowly drifted further away, pulled by the sluggish current of the slimy water.

"Darn," thought Doug. "Why won't you swim this way?"

He stood up. "Maybe if I can get to that rock, I can catch him from there."

Cautiously he moved his foot along the log, holding his breath so that the frog would not be frightened into diving. As he moved, he unwittingly let his weight shift onto a very badly rotted section of the wood. Slowly it sank away beneath him, and Doug looked frantically around for support. But there was none. With a soft, squishy splash he slid up to his knees in the mud and water. With ooze sucking at his legs, and no sure footing on the greasy bottom, he suddenly found himself sitting, waist-deep in slime.

"Mom will kill me," he thought, dragging himself onto the bank. Even though his clothes were not new, nor even very clean, his mother would be almost certain to forbid further frog-hunting expeditions. She might not even let him play with Paul after this!

Paul? Where was he? He would know what to do. Doug had to catch up with his friend.

"Wait up, Paul!" His shout brought no answer. It was darker now than he had thought. A cloud had probably blocked off the afternoon sun.

Scrambling along the bank, with one foot sliding back into the water again, he reached the path. Awkwardly he

clambered up the shallow cliff, and, on dry ground at last, sat panting on the trail all the children used when they visited The Bush.

He stared absently for a few moments at the water. Once trains had drawn water from the pond to fill the boilers for their engines. The tracks were only about fifty metres away; Doug could see the gravelled slope of the roadbed through a gap in the cedars. His father had told him that long ago the pond had been used for swimming, and boys had even been able to fish there.

Doug had always doubted these "fish stories", and now, having had his own dip in the stagnant pool, he was convinced that swimming could never have been possible there, either.

But his father had insisted about the fish. When the railway used the pond, it was deeper, he said. Water ran from the pond over a dam at one end. The concrete parts of the dam were still there, but the log barrier, made from railway ties, had either rotted or been washed away. There used to be a waterfall, his father told him—now only a tiny trickle slithered out of the pond between the two concrete edges of the old dam.

There were no more fish—even frogs were difficult to find. The water came in from two slender creeks. One, wandering north through the fields, had never been traced to its source by anyone that Doug knew. The other came from a pipe at the factory.

Suddenly, Doug remembered Paul. Jumping to his

feet, he dashed along the path to the field, expecting to see his friend almost at the road by this time. He called as loudly as he could, but there was no reply. In front of him, the trail reached the edge of The Bush, and opened onto a stretch of meadow.

The field reached ahead for perhaps several hundred metres, overgrown already with dandelion and chickory, until it splashed its weeds against the shoulder of a road. Across the road was the factory, and, beyond that, the houses where his and Paul's families lived. Even farther on was the town, where the rest of their friends lived, and where they went to school.

Doug squinted over the rippling field. It was brighter than it had been under the trees, and his eyes took their time adjusting to the change; but even so the light was somehow less than he had expected.

No Paul in the field. No Paul on the road, or across the road. No Paul anywhere.

Doug felt lost. His friend was a year older than he, and would have known exactly how to deal with cold, soggy, ill-smelling clothes; and, much more importantly, how to explain to his angry mother what had happened. Doug ran his sleeve across his nose as he felt tears forming in his eyes. He sat down under the huge ancient beech tree that guarded the path's entry to The Bush. He had to solve this problem alone, now, but what should be done?

"I'll tell her just what happened. Maybe she won't let me come here again, but she might change her mind.

After all, it's not Paul's fault. He wanted me to come for supper. If I tell her that, she will still let me play with Paul."

A tiny movement on his right found a reflection in his tear-filled eye. Doug turned his head to see a large brown mouse squatting on a rock near him.

"No, it's a chipmunk," he murmured. As he watched, it even looked something like a bat, but he knew bats don't stand upright; they hang upside-down from their perches. He blinked.

Now his eyes were clear enough for him to realize that the tiny brown creature was a little man, dressed in fur from his head to his knees with a skin cape hanging from his shoulders. When he moved his arms, the cape looked like a bat's wings. The man's face and limbs were a very dark, chestnut brown, and he wore a shaggy beard. He was about twenty centimetres tall, and stood gazing at Doug, his left arm stretched out, and holding a slim pointed stick that might have been a spear. He looked like a little warrior.

"Who are you?" Doug did not know whether to be afraid or friendly, but curiosity was blazing inside him.

The little man continued to stare at Doug. Then the boy heard a deeper, darker voice than he had expected. The reply was as puzzling as the creature itself.

CHAPTER TWO
ULOC

"I have no name," it answered. "The first men, the hunters who roamed this land for many thousands of years, called me *Ah-cha-pai*, The Changer, for they saw me in many forms. Then the new men, with light skins and bright axes, did not at first see me at all. When they did, they called me Elf, or Leprechaun, or Spirit. I am none of these. I am the guardian of this pond, which was once a deep pool on a free, sweet stream, the home of trout and salmon, of turtle and muskrat, mink and otter."

"Boy! Then Dad was right," stammered Doug. "They did catch fish in the railway pond!"

"Pond?" asked the little figure. "Who speaks of ponds? I was the guardian of a pool in a free-flowing stream—the men of the iron trail built a prison for my stream, but still I could roar, still I could thunder out of prison when the spring sun fed my stream with melted snow. Once their iron trail itself was overcome by my waters.

"But now, my stream is dying. Men rob my stream of water for the great smoking houses they have built in the land just north of here. In return they give me the filth from the great house beyond the grass."

"You mean the factory," gasped Doug. "That's where Paul's father works."

"Their poison has killed my fish and my turtles; and the mink and the otter and the muskrat have fled to other rivers. I am left alone here with a few frogs in a dying swamp. Even my frogs grow fewer every spring."

The little man paused sadly, as if thinking of what used to be. Then, suddenly looking at Doug, he said: "That is why you must help me. You are the only one I can trust."

"Me!" exclaimed Doug. "You don't even know who I am. What can I do to help you?"

"I have watched you many times when you have come to the pond. You are called Doug. You are quieter than your friends; you think more, and you feel more. You love even this last bit of my stream. You have never killed the smallest of my creatures. You know many of my secrets and you have kept them to yourself. Friends do not tell secrets to those they do not trust. And, in a way, you, too, have suffered from the changes forced on my

12

stream. Many years ago, a slip into my water would have brought laughter, not tears.

"And you can see me—as I really am. But, most of all, my spear tells me I can trust you."

"What do you mean, 'see you'? Can't everyone see you, if they look?"

"Only those who care can see me," replied the tiny figure. Most children, and almost all grown-ups, see a mouse, a stone, a stump, a bat, a chunk of earth—but they don't see *me*, for there is no real love of my pool in their hearts."

"Has no one ever seen you before?"

"Many have seen me."

"Why haven't they told others about you?"

"Some have. Most have promised not to tell of me, and have kept their word. Those who broke their pledge and tried to convince others, hoping to help perhaps, got only scorn and disbelief as their reward. It is many years since I have been seen."

"Believers were simpler to find in the days of the hunting men, the first people. They loved my stream and the land around it. They were ready to believe me. Today few people come here who want to find me or my creatures in peace. I think you to be one of those few. Will you help me?"

"How can I help you, Mr. ......? What was your name again?"

"You may name me Uloc, which in my language

means 'first', for I was here long before men hunted the forest or cut the trees."

"You must be very, very old, Uloc. Will you ever die?"

"Without my amulet, I will die when this stream is gone. That is why I need you."

"What is an amulet? How can I help?"

"My amulet is a piece of jade, a pale green stone shaped like the full moon and smoothed by the rushing waters of a thousand springtimes. If you look into it, you may see a trout flashing, smell the freshness of wild flowers, hear beechnuts falling to the forest soil, or feel the bite of snow lashed across a faded winter moon. I have always had my stone, and may not leave this stream without it. It came from the stream and when the stream is gone, my amulet is all that will remain of it—and me.

"But now, it has disappeared. Someone must have taken it while I was careless in guarding the pond. It has been gone now for almost a year, and I have searched all over the woods with no success. You must look for it beyond the trees or I shall perish, poisoned with my frogs in a stream I cannot leave."

"Why don't you just go without it? What will happen?"

"There are many other, cleaner streams in this land, but I cannot leave this one without my amulet. I have tried many times, yet I cannot break through into the outer world without it. If I go past this place into the grass, I am stopped. It is as though invisible ropes hold

14

me back. It is part of the Old Order of the world, and cannot be changed. You must find the amulet, or I am doomed. There is no other answer. Will you try?"

Doug squirmed uneasily. He had no hope of finding a little piece of green stone alone in a world thousands of kilometres across. He felt something like resentment against Uloc for selecting him, for making him feel some responsibility for the little man's sufferings. If Uloc died, Doug knew he would be partly to blame. Why did he have to be the one?

"Will you?"

"I will try my best, Uloc, but I don't think it will be any use. If someone took your jade, he will have hidden it. I can't look everywhere, you know."

"You can only try, my friend. I do not ask the impossible, only the difficult. Do you also promise to tell no one about me?"

"Not even Paul?"

"Do you trust him?"

"Yes, Uloc."

"Then I, too, will trust him. You may tell him, but he will not believe you until he sees me. Bring him here tomorrow."

The little man removed his cloak. Handing it to Doug, he proclaimed. "This cape has a special gift. When you wear it, you have only to wish to see me, and you will be here."

"It's too small for me to wear," Doug protested.

"Place it on your shoulder. Take the spear also. If you carry it, you will be able to tell whether men mean what they say; you will know if they are lying or joking or speaking the truth. It told me about you and will tell you about others. I am grateful for your kindness."

As he spoke, Uloc stepped back beside the tree and faded away.

Looking up, Doug noticed lights in his house.

"Gosh, I'd better hurry. I'll get a licking for sure, now."

And he raced across the field towards home.

CHAPTER THREE
NEW PROBLEMS FOR DOUG

Doug stole along the path to the side door. The kitchen lights were burning, but the station wagon was not in the driveway.

"Maybe Dad is late for supper, too," he thought. "Mom will be twice as angry about my clothes."

He timidly pulled open the screen door, announcing his presence with a faint, questioning call: "Mom?"

Silence.

Growing slightly (ever so slightly) more venturesome, Doug carefully made his way up the stairs into the kitchen. The room was empty, and the rest of the house was filled with the kind of quiet that fills vacant spaces at dusk. Propped up against the salt shaker on the kitchen table was a note.

HI DOUG,

WE'VE TAKEN ANN OVER TO KATHY'S TO SPEND THE NIGHT. WILL BE BACK SOON. BE GOOD.

DAD.

"Oh, boy I'm in luck." Now he had time to change his clothes, and, what was even better, Ann would not be there to hear about her older brother's problems.

After a brief struggle with the drawer, he dug out clean jeans, socks, and underwear. There was a new shirt in the closet. He bundled up his dirty clothes and dropped them down the laundry chute on his way to the shower. This was one time when he would not require hounding about the use of soap.

He dried, dressed, and sat down to plan the best approach. A car pulling into the drive, followed by footsteps and the stretching metal sound of the aluminum screen door, warned him that his parents had returned. He walked through to meet them.

"Hi Mom. Hi Dad."

"Hello Dougie. Why have you changed your clothes?" The dreaded enquiry!

"I fell in some dirty water and made a mess of the others. I put them in the laundry."

"That's a good boy, Dougie." His mother was not even annoyed. She was too busy scrambling through the cupboards gathering ingredients and utensils for supper.

"Are you good and hungry? I'm going to make lots of

spaghetti for your Dad and you."

"Yum," drooled Doug.

All through dinner his mother fired questions at Dad.

"How big is their tent?

"How long will it take?

"How much food do I pack?"

Doug was temporarily mystified, but between questions, his parents unfolded a change in their vacation plans. They were not just staying home after all.

"We're going on a camping trip through Northern Ontario," his father announced. "Your Mom and I used to do a lot of camping, and we decided it was time to start again. We'll be a little rusty at it, but you and Ann will be able to help. As soon as school ends next Friday, we can leave. Sound all right to you, son?"

"Wow!" whooped Doug. "That's terrific! I've never been camping way out in the forest before. Can we canoe? There are lots of animals, I'll bet! Can I light the fires?"

"Hold on, Doug. Your Dad and I haven't made all the plans yet. You and Ann have to share that job with us."

"Did you buy a tent, Dad?"

"We borrowed the big green wall tent from the Jamiesons. They don't need it until August. We can use most of their camping gear as well. You have your own sleeping bag, Ann has hers at Kathy's right now, and your Mom and I will get ours. If we plan carefully, we might get as far north as Timmins."

Doug was so excited he could hardly finish his spaghetti; he even had to be coaxed into dessert.

After supper, Doug cleared the table faster than he had ever done before.

"Can I go next door to tell Paul about our trip?" he pleaded.

"Be back by eight o'clock," his father ordered.

Doug bounded out the side door, rounded the back of the house, and ran to his friend's.

As he reached the door, a dreadful realization suddenly cut into his excitement. Uloc! He had promised to find the jade, or at least to do his best. Would he break the pledge by going away? Would Uloc still be here when he came home? It would be his fault if he were not.

He rapped on the door. Paul would know what to do.

"Hi Doug. Catch the frog?"

"No, I fell in the pond. Don't laugh like that. It sure smelled terrible."

"I can't help it. Come on in and see the new model space capsule my Dad bought for me. I'm halfway finished building it."

Doug was led to his friend's room, where he admired the plastic satellite. Paul had been fascinated by space travel ever since Doug could remember, following American and Russian moon landings, and clipping all the newspapers for his "space scrapbook". The new model was one that Paul had wanted for almost a year, and he was enormously proud of it.

After admiring Paul's new satellite, Doug changed the subject with some hesitation.

"Paul, I've got a problem. My Dad is taking us camping next week."

"What's the problem? I'd love to go camping. Trade places with me!"

"That's not the bad part. You see, I made a promise to someone." He told Paul about his meeting with Uloc in The Bush, and explained the task he had accepted.

"Don't be silly, Dougie." Paul called him Dougie only when he wanted to remind Doug that he was a year older and wiser.

"You can't fool anyone with an idiotic story like that. Don't muck up your trip with a stupid lie. Did you tell your folks that story?"

"No, I promised Uloc I would just tell you. He said nobody would believe me."

"Well, he was right, starting with me. I really am surprised at you, Dougie."

Doug was annoyed by his friend's disbelief, and Paul's grown-up manner made him furious.

"Come on. I'll prove it's true!" he shouted. "Come and see the spear and cloak he gave me. They're magic."

"They'll have to be, to convince me."

The boys went back to Doug's house and climbed the stairs to the bedroom. "There, on the bed, know-it-all."

"Where on the bed?"

Doug gasped. The spear and cloak were gone.

"I put them there when I came in."

"All I can see is a pair of old sneakers, there on the floor. Those must be the ones you wore today. They're still wet."

Doug stared at the shoes.

"Why don't you give up, Dougie? You've had your fun. There's no magic sword or cloak."

"It was a *spear*, and I put it there on the bed." If Paul had not been with him, Doug would have cried.

Everything, it now seemed to him, had been only a dream.

CHAPTER FOUR
PAUL CONVINCED

Doug awoke next morning to a day that seemed determined to set new records for sunshine. Pleasanter yet, it was the Saturday before the last week of school.

But Doug could think only of the loss of the magic gifts. Had someone stolen them? Or was the whole adventure unreal, something he had imagined? Maybe the pond had some funny chemicals in it that made people see and hear things no one else could.

He pulled on shorts and a T-shirt and stumbled out to the kitchen. He had to hurry, to get back to The Bush. Perhaps he had dropped the gifts on his way home.

He had finished his orange juice and a bowl of cereal when his mother arrived, demanding he eat some toast as well, before he brushed his teeth.

"When you are all cleaned up, come to me for inspection. Ann wants her white shorts for this afternoon, so I'll be downstairs, doing the laundry. At least I won't have to wash again Monday."

"Will do, Mom."

As soon as the toast had joined the juice and cereal, Doug shot into the bathroom to wash and brush. He finished, made his bed (his hurry prevented a very neat job), and stuck his feet into yesterday's now-dry sneakers. Off he went to find Mom.

"I'm going to The Bush, Mom."

His mother, busily sorting clothes to be bleached from those not to be bleached, did not hear him. The thrashing of the old washing-machine was too loud. He would have to move closer.

"I'm going to the .... hey!" Doug grabbed at the thin piece of leather that fell from the bundle of clothes his mother had picked up—the same bundle he had dropped down the chute yesterday.

"I need this. Is there a spear, too?"

"Yes, and a vicious weapon it is. It just jabbed me in the arm. You should warn your poor mother about the booby-traps in your clothing." She handed him the pointed stick.

"I'm going to Paul's, Mom. Then we might go up through the fields."

"Be back for lunch. Your father may take us out for a hamburger, with French fries."

"Okay." The side door banged shut behind Doug's heels. Wait until Paul saw these!

"Paul! Hey, Paul! Look! I found them!" Paul was digging under the spruce trees behind his house.

"Found what, Doug?"

"The gifts," said Doug. "The one I told you about last night, and couldn't find. The spear and the cloak."

"All right, magician, show Paul your tricks." Paul obviously did not believe him.

"There aren't any tricks, Paul, only magic. Like when I put this cloak on my shoulder, and wish I were with Uloc, I *am* there."

"Ha! Don't be silly. You mean if you put it on you like this, and speak your wish, you fly through the air? Baloney, Dougie."

"I'm sorry I ever told you about Uloc. I'd rather talk to him than to you," said Doug, angrily taking the cloak back.

Even while he spoke the sentence, Doug could see Paul and the spruce branches first begin to melt, then vanish. In their place were the grey beech trunk and the rock. On the rock stood Uloc.

"What do you need, Doug? Did you find the stone?"

"No, Uloc. Paul will not believe me. I don't know what to do."

"Paul will believe you now. Bring him to see me."

Doug set off through the field. In the distance he could see Paul standing in his backyard. When Paul saw Doug, he ran to meet him.

27

"What happened, Doug? How did you do that?"

"Come on. Uloc's in The Bush. He wants to see you, now!"

Paul followed Doug without questioning or laughing this time. Across the road, through the field, right to the beech tree.

"Shush, Doug! Look at the little squirrel on the rock! Hey, that's not a squirrel, it's a . . . . a . . . . What is it?"

"It's Uloc. See his beard? His arms are crossed over his chest. Look closely, Paul."

"I can't really see; it's all fuzzy . . . . Wait, I can see him now."

"You need be in no hurry, boy," said Uloc. "I have seen you many times."

"Doug told me about you, but I thought he was just making it up. I was wrong. I'm sorry, Doug."

"I have a question, Uloc," interrupted Doug. "I thought of it when I was lying in bed last night.

"If you are the guardian of the pool, why don't you stop people from ruining the stream? What can you do to guard the stream if you can't stop the bad things from happening?"

"It is part of the Old Order, my friend. I guard the pool against Evil. I kept the pool deep to protect it from *Ga-Nakawasis*, Lord of Drought, and to prevent his sons, *Pitaki*, Lord of Thirst and *Satika*, Lord of Hunger, from harming my creatures. I defied Ga-Nakawasis for many centuries, protecting the deer for the hunting men and . . the cattle for the land-breaking men. Without me and

28

my thousand thousand brothers throughout the world, men would fall before *Tau*, Lord of Hatred and *Ba-Kasis*, Lord of Despair. From all these creatures of Evil I have guarded men by guarding my pool."

"But why could you not protect it from the men who spoiled it?"

"I can only protect it from evil beings; the men who are destroying it are not evil. They are merely foolish, or thoughtless, or lazy; but they are *not* wicked. They thought they were doing the right thing, the very necessary thing. They were trying to make many things better, but they have failed. Their failure has destroyed my stream, and may yet destroy mankind. But very seldom do men become truly evil. They are not possessed by Evil—only by a mistaken idea of progress that will benefit all men. In the end, they may destroy my stream. And since my amulet is, in a way, all that remains of the stream of the Old Order, it must be found."

"Doug said we had to find your amulet. Where was it when it was stolen from you?"

"It was beneath the rock on which I now stand. It has been kept there from the very beginning. Then, one day, the rock was lifted up and my jade, was gone.

"When was it taken?"

"When the last moon of spring shone, four seasons past."

"That would be last May," said Paul thoughtfully. Then he added, "Let's not sit here uselessly. Let's find the jade."

30

CHAPTER FIVE
HELP SNEAKS IN

Doug's father invited Paul to come with them to the drive-in restaurant. The boys sat together on a heavily-initialled bench, dripping ketchup from their hamburgers and planning their quest for the missing jade.

"This afternoon we can search the field across from your Dad's factory," suggested Doug.

"Yeah. That will be a pretty big job. One little green pebble in all that green grass. Some of those weeds come up to my shoulder."

"Bring your milkshakes, you two!" called Dad. "We have to collect Ann by two o'clock!"

Herded into the back seat of the station wagon, the pair fell silent and watched the traffic in the other lane.

Ann and her friend Kathy were on the front porch,

waiting for the car. Doug groaned at his sister's bouncing approach.

Before long, Ann had said goodbye to Kathy, stowed her gear, and launched into a minute-by-minute report of the visit. Although he would never admit it, Doug enjoyed his sister's chattering. Ann was many things that Doug had never been: she was noisy; she moved her whole body constantly; she had dozens of friends. Everyone liked Ann.

Doug was occasionally jealous of his sister, especially when she was invited to places, but he always tolerated, usually liked, and sometimes even admired her.

" . . . . And Kathy swung her pillow at me, but she hit the box of powder. It was all over the floor, but we put most of it back and swept up the rest. It was loads of laughs, Mom."

Ann always filled the car with words and giggles. It seemed that she was never really quiet. The narrative lasted throughout the entire homeward journey. The moment the car stopped in Doug's driveway, the boys bolted out.

" 'Bye, Mom. 'Bye, Dad."

"Thanks for the hamburger and stuff, Mr. Torrance. See you later, Ann. 'Bye!"

"Where are you going, Dougie?"

"To the field, Mom. I'll be back by supper."

The factory was silent as they passed. All the machinery was shut off for the weekend. Paul said that lots of factories had machines that never stopped, but his father (who was manager) made sure that all the switches were off every night, and stayed off on Saturdays and Sundays.

After wandering at random through the grass, the boys decided that they would have to search in a pattern if they hoped to find anything.

"Let's walk across the field from the path to that fence, and then back. That way we can't look twice in the same place."

"Good idea. Let's check along the pathway first, just in case."

The plan was put into action. As each strip was searched, they tied a handful of grass in a knot on the fence to make certain they did not retrace their steps.

"Boy, this is really boring, Doug," moaned Paul as they finished the first half of the field.

"How can we hope to find a little tiny chunk of green jade in all of these weeds? It's worse than fishing for a dime in the lining of your jeans. I don't even think that the stone is in the field, Paul."

"Ted Kirkman has a green stone." The boys were startled by Ann's voice in the tall grass next to them.

"What are you doing here? Spying on us? Who invited you?"

"I wanted to see what you and Paul were doing. I have nobody to play with, and Mom's busy."

"How do you know Ted has a piece of jade?"

"Is that a green kind of stone? His sister, Lisa, showed

it to me at school last winter. She borrowed it without asking. She always does that, and wow, does he get mad!"

"I wonder if it's *the* jade—the amulet, I mean? What did it look like, Ann?"

"It was round, like a ball, or maybe a teeny bit egg-shaped. It was so shiny and smooth that you could almost see pictures in it, sort of like a mirror."

"That must be it, Doug. How do we get it from Ted?"

"We just take it. He stole it from Uloc, didn't he?"

"Who's Uloc, Dougie? What do you mean, Ted stole it? Lisa said he found it in The Bush. I was going to look for more, but I forgot, once the snow was gone."

"You and your big mouth, Doug. Didn't you promise You-Know-Who not to tell anyone but me? Now your sister will spread the whole secret all over town."

"You're right. I've spoiled everything now."

"I *will not* spread your silly secret," objected Ann. "Especially since you haven't told me anything yet. Who's Uloc? What's all this about a secret?"

"What will we do, Paul?"

"You go ask You-Know-Who what to do. I'll wait here with the girl."

"My name is Ann, not 'the girl'!"

Doug left them to argue over Ann's title, and waded through the field to the beech tree. Sure that his sister would see nothing, he began calling softly.

"Uloc, where are you? Uloc, we need help. Uloc!

Uloc!"

"What news, friend?" asked a dark, gruff voice.

"Where are you?"

"Up here." Doug glanced into the branches and saw Uloc sitting astride a bough about a metre over his head.

"Uloc, we think we know who has the jade."

"Excellent, Doug," cried Uloc floating down from his perch like an autumn leaf. "Who is it?"

"A boy named Ted found it. We can maybe get it back for you on Monday. I don't know where he lives, so I'll have to ask him at school."

"Why did you say you needed help? Will he not give it up willingly?"

"Oh, I don't know, I need help because my sister found out about you. She sneaked up when Paul and I were talking about you and listened to us."

"That is not true, Doug. I am holding another of my spears. It tells me that you bend your story."

"Well, I guess I did know she was there when I said your name. It was Ann who told us where the jade was."

"Then she is with us. I would like to meet this maiden. Will she come to me? I cannot go to her until I again have the stone."

"She'll be delighted, Uloc. But she talks a lot. Do you think the secret will be safe?"

"Apparently as safe as with you, my friend. Please ask her to come."

"Paul! Ann!" shouted Doug as he crashed through the chickory. "Come here! It's all right!"

Strangely enough, when they reached the tree, Ann saw Uloc almost at once. For a second she stared at a large piece of shaggy bark, then suddenly gasped, "It's a man! A little wee man!"

"Yes, daughter. Can you guard a secret from enemies?....Good." Uloc began to tell the story, with Doug and Paul anxiously adding scraps of information whenever they could politely interrupt him.

"So now I have three allies," finished Uloc. "The goal is very near. You have saved us much time, little maiden."

"I only hope Ted still has the stone," added Doug. "And that he'll give it to us."

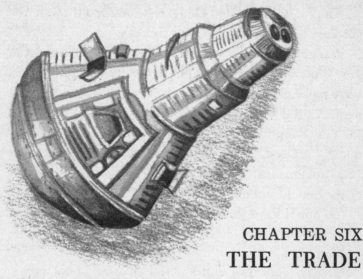

CHAPTER SIX
THE TRADE

Sunday brought a new round of excitement. During a planning session for the camping trip, Doug had asked if Paul could come along.

"He'll have to ask his parents, Doug. But it's fine with us," his father replied. "Or better still, I'll call his Dad and check. No sense in getting Paul all excited if he can't go, is there?"

Doug was so surprised by his parent's answer that he could only sit grinning while his father telephoned.

"Dad and I had already talked about inviting Paul," his mother explained. "We thought it might be a good idea, because you always seem so, well . . . . ."

Doug knew the rest of the sentence. He had overheard his parents talking several times. "Dougie always seems so lonely. Except for Paul, there are no children near him. Maybe we should move into town." Doug had never really wanted to move, and now that Paul was coming camping, there was nothing further needed for perfect happiness.

"Dad thought you should be the one to bring up the idea, though, so we said nothing."

His father strode back into the room and sent Doug next door to break the good news to Paul. "His father said he'll be glad to get rid of him for two weeks. I think he was joking, but maybe we're in for a rough time with young Paul along," laughed Dad.

In his excitement, Doug missed these words. He and Paul spent the rest of the afternoon planning how to search for roots and berries, what to do if they saw a bear, and where to set the tent in relation to trees and rocks.

That evening, their excited discussion continued while Paul finished his model space capsule. Tremendous care went into its construction, and when the decals were in place it looked to the boys like a genuine masterpiece.

They were still discussing plans as they straggled to school on Monday. It was going to be a blazing hot day, and both were in favour of leaving for the camping trip immediately.

"Don't forget about Ted," panted Ann as she caught up with them.

"We won't," replied Doug. "It's at the top of our list of things to do before we leave. See?" He shoved a piece

of blue paper at her.

1. GET THE JADE.
2. PACK CLOTHES.
3. GET FISHING TACKLE READY.
4. AIR OUT SLEEPING BAGS.

In the schoolyard, Paul and Doug started off to find
Ted. Ann, besieged by a multitude of friends, was
whisked away.

"What's in the other bag, Paul? Another lunch?"

"I brought my space capsule to show the class this
morning. I'm taking it back home after school. Look,
there's Ted!"

At first, Ted did not understand what the two wanted.
When he finally knew what the jade was, he answered
casually. "Oh, the green rock. I traded it to Kevin for
thirty-five marbles last Easter. You'll have to ask him."

"Where did you find it, Ted?"

"Up by the railway tracks, a long time ago, when I was
looking for salamanders. I turned over a big, flat stone,
and there it was. I never did get the salamanders. They
were going to be for my science project. Anyway, this
dumb little stone wasn't much use as a marble; it
wouldn't roll straight. But Kevin thought it looked inter-
esting, so he gave me all those alleys for it."

"Well, thanks anyway, Ted. Let's go see Kev."

Kevin Lang was practising at the high-jump pit, and
had just knocked off the bar.

"Kevin, we have to ask you something," called Doug.

"What do you want, Little One?" sneered Kevin, who was in Paul's class.

"Have you still got that green stone Ted traded you for all those marbles?"

"Yeah. It's in my rock collection at home. It's a piece of jade. That's a gemstone; pretty valuable. Ted thinks he outsmarted me, but I got the best part of that deal."

"Oh, Oh," thought Paul. "He's not going to just give it to us."

"I'll give you fifty marbles if you'll let me have it," offered Doug.

"Are you crazy? It's worth a lot more than that, Little One. I know about rocks."

"I'll give you all my marbles."

"Get lost, Dougie."

"All the marbles and ten comic books?"

"Beat it."

"And my Matchbox Model A Ford? That would be a good deal."

"Don't make funnies, kid. Leave me alone. I have to practise my high jump." Kevin was entered in the track meet the following day.

The bell rang. Surrounded by children surging towards the school, the two friends plodded gloomily across the playground.

"What will we do, Paul? He won't trade us the jade. We can't get it any other way."

"I don't know. I'll talk to you at recess."

Doug was not in good spirits for spelling, and he remained despondent even during mathematics, his favourite subject. He kept wondering how to get the jade back. When he answered that seven times six was thirteen, the whole class giggled, but he was not bothered by their laughter. He had greater worries.

At last came recess. He hurried outside to find Paul, but his friend was nowhere to be seen. Finally Doug saw him, reluctantly dragging his feet along the side walkway.

"What's wrong, Paul? Are you sick?"

"I got the jade, Doug. He'll bring it this afternoon."

"Wow, that's great! Does he want my marbles and stuff?"

"No."

"Well, he didn't just give it to you, did he? What does he want?"

"My space capsule."

CHAPTER SEVEN
THE UNINVITED GUEST

Paul handed over his prized model that afternoon and received the jade. Gazing into the misty green gem, Doug and Ann were sure they saw many constantly-changing images in the depths, but Paul was unconvinced.

"I can only see my capsule," he lamented.

"You can have all that neat junk I offered to trade Kevin, if you want it." Doug's attempt to comfort his friend met no success.

"Let's take this thing to Uloc," Paul muttered. They stopped only to tell their mothers where they were going. They barrelled past the factory and along the path through the field, arriving breathless at the beech tree. Uloc was waiting for them.

"I can feel it already," he shouted. "You have the

amulet, you have found it! Its power and strength are coming back to me."

Paul handed him the stone.

"You are the most excellent of friends, children. I am indebted to you to the end of all seasons. My only regret is that I have nothing to offer you. For the moment, I offer only my blessing, the poor blessing of the guardian of a dying stream. Still, it takes away all fear and hatred of water, and gives love of its beauty and respect for its danger."

"That's a good blessing, Uloc. My Dad says that where we are going to camp we will see some of the most beautiful water and rock in the whole world."

"Eh? Where are you going?" Uloc's eyes sparkled with interest.

"We're going up into Northern Ontario, where my Dad says the small lakes are ten times the size of the Mill Pond, and where there's a lake so huge you could sink a whole country in it. I can't remember which country, though."

"So you travel north, children, to the land of free streams and the cleanest of waters." His eyes were now flaming. "I will accompany you on your journey. Many years have I yearned to make this trip, but I was afraid to go unguided. All my days I have never gone more than a few hours away from this spot. Now I can."

Doug's mouth gaped. He couldn't really have heard properly. "But .... but ...." he spluttered, "we can't take you .... Mom and Dad would say no."

"They will not see me. To a grown-up, I am a mouse, a squirrel, a bat."

"Oh, swell," moaned Ann. "Just what Mom needs, a camping trip with a giant mouse! She doesn't even like regulation-size mice. It won't work, Uloc. We couldn't take you; we really couldn't."

"You might hide me, so I would never be seen."

"Where could we hide you?"

"Under the car seat," offered Paul. "He would fit under your Dad's seat. Your Mom wouldn't be frightened if she never saw him, would she?"

"Well said," applauded Uloc.

"It doesn't sound honest to me, sneaking Uloc under a car seat and hiding him from Mom and Dad. Couldn't we tell them, Dougie?" asked Ann.

"I think they would agree if they could see Uloc as he really is and if they knew the whole story. But, it's not exactly cheating or lying to hide Uloc, because he's already hidden from them. Can you make yourself look like a rock or a stick instead of a mouse, Uloc?"

"My shape depends on the person who sees me. All men see me as they want to, and I cannot control how I look to them. Perhaps they will see me as a stick, perhaps not."

"I guess we'll have to risk your being seen, then. How about it, Ann? It might be fun to have Uloc with us, don't you think?"

"Oh, sure," his sister answered doubtfully. "I just hope Mom doesn't hit him with the axe when she finds him in a sleeping bag."

46

"I shall find my own lodging once we arrive," was Uloc's cool reply. "I ask only that you take me on the journey."

At length, all three children agreed. Uloc promised solemnly to stay out of sight, to keep away from the campsite, and not to steal food.

"What do you eat out here, anyway, Uloc?" asked Paul.

"That, too, is part of the Old Order."

"Very mysterious indeed," thought Paul to himself. "Probably bugs and things." He looked at the little man with great pity as he considered such a diet.

The children promised to fetch Uloc before the trip, but he had apparently decided to go with them immediately, and set up housekeeping in Paul's backyard. ("I never even invited him," muttered Paul, "not that it would make any difference to him, I suppose.")

They set off dismally across the field, except for Uloc, who marched along, singing songs in the strange language, with a deep, ancient voice. As they neared the two houses, however, even Uloc fell silent.

"I will stay beneath the spruce trees, my friends. I am at your call." He melted away into the spruce root before their eyes could follow his disappearance.

"Well, I guess no one will see him if we can't, eh Doug?"

"I wonder where he goes to?"

"I stand here before you," replied Uloc's voice. "You have only to look."

"I still can't see you."

"Neither can I."

"Then it is as you wished, children. Summon me if you need."

It was suppertime for Ann and Doug. Paul went in to read the comic page.

Uloc had vanished so completely that the children scarcely thought of him until Thursday evening, when Doug heard his mother searching in the kitchen cupboards.

"Dougie, did you eat those peanuts we had left? I can't find them."

"They're on the second shelf, Mom." It was Ann who replied.

"Oh, yes. There's a squirrel on the back lawn. I'm going to feed him. Want to help, you two?"

"Oh, boy," cried Ann, following her mother out the side door.

Doug had hardly heard the door shut when Ann's excited voice and racing footsteps alerted him.

"Doug! Doug, what will we do? It's not a squirrel! It's Uloc! Think of something. What will we say to Mom?"

"Come on." Doug headed for Ann's bedroom window. From there they could see the back lawn.

"Look, Ann!"

There was Mom, crouching in the most undignified manner, pelting Uloc with peanuts. Uloc was standing placidly, his arms folded firmly under his beard. His face was a mixture of pleasure and amazement. He picked up one of the nearest peanuts, walked hurriedly to Paul's tree, and vanished.

"Oh, no," gasped Doug. "He promised to stay out of sight."

"Don't you children like squirrels?" Mom was in the kitchen again. "I'm glad he's moved in next door. It makes me feel closer to the countryside in spite of the factory. He certainly enjoyed those peanuts."

Ann looked at Doug. Mom had fed Uloc nuts without seeing his true shape. Not only that, she even liked him.

"I have a feeling we'll see a lot of that squirrel, children."

But the children were already in Paul's yard.

"Uloc!" they called. "Oh, there you are! You promised to stay hidden. Why did you let Mom see you?"

"Ah, your mother. A generous and thoughtful lady, Doug. But she did not see me. I have kept my word, have I not? Your mother did not see me—Uloc—for even one instant."

Ann was astonished. "I guess that's true, but please, Uloc, stay in the tree, will you?"

"I shall try, maiden. Return this nut to your mother if you wish. I do not eat them, but I did not like to offend her generosity."

"Just wait here, Uloc. We are leaving early Saturday morning. We have everything packed already."

"I am most anxious to set out." The words seemed to come from the spruce root.

The children shared the peanut as they walked back to the house.

CHAPTER EIGHT
THE TRIP

Doug's room was still dark when he woke Saturday morning. He dressed quickly and made his bed. There was no sense in delaying the departure time.

He slipped into the living room to read until the rest of the family was awake. When his mother got up to make breakfast, she found him stretched out on the sofa, fast asleep.

As they finished the meal, Paul arrived at the door. All his luggage had been packed away the previous evening, so he had only to hop into the car.

"All set to blast off, neighbour?" asked Dad.

"All set," grinned Paul.

"Why don't you go get in the car, Paul? I'll send these three out to join you as soon as they're ready. The little ones are no problem, but it may take some effort to get Mrs. Torrance prepared." He smiled at his wife.

"It's a mother's duty to check everything carefully before leaving. You wouldn't want the stove left on, would you?"

Paul signalled to Doug to come to the door. "Uloc's in the roses. Shall I put him under the seat?"

"Yes. Ann fixed up a cornflakes box with cloth and stuff for him to lie in. Perhaps he'll go to sleep."

Paul scampered off to install the stowaway.

When Doug joined his friend in the back seat of the station wagon, he pushed something under the seat beside the cornflakes box prepared by Ann.

"What's that?" asked Paul.

"The cloak and spear. If we're not going to see Uloc again, I'd better return his things. He might need them in

his new home. Have you got your amulet, Uloc?"

"It is in the pouch at my side. The cave is fitted with every comfort, my friends. The journey will be pleasant."

Ann entered the car. "Uloc likes your invention," reported her brother.

The three children waited impatiently until finally Mom and Dad appeared on the porch and locked the front door. Mom was still mentally checking her list-of-things-to-be-sure-to-do.

"We'll follow Highway 400 until it joins 11. Then we take 11 right through, almost to Timmins."

For the first few kilometres, the children eagerly examined the passing landscapes, commenting on each outstanding feature, whether cow, car, or cornfield. But soon they lapsed into a drowsy state, half-watching,

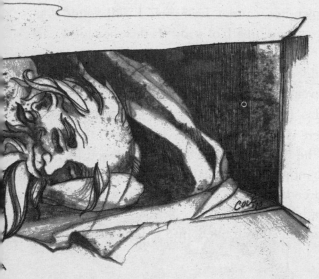

half-dozing. The one who saw onions growing in the black soil, or who noticed canal or radio broadcast tower had almost to rouse the other two to point it out. When Paul peeked into Uloc's "cave", he saw the little man breathing deeply, his eyes shut.

The morning passed. South of Gravenhurst, the travellers stopped for lunch, resuming the journey after a picnic meal and a lot of leg-stretching. Huge rocks now hemmed in the highway at many points, while great expanses of water or forest stretched off at others.

"These are some of the oldest rock formations in the country, children, part of the Canadian Shield," Dad informed them.

"The oldest?" The three children were shocked to hear Uloc's voice. Ann, who was closest to him tried to shush him up, but he would not be silenced.

"The grown-ups cannot hear me. I will sound like rustling leaves, or a breath of wind. Is this the oldest part of the land?"

Doug nodded anixously. His parents would be able to hear *him*, even if Uloc was soundless.

"Then this is where I will begin to seek my new stream. There is a very ancient saying, 'From the oldest shall come the new.' I never before understood its message." Uloc returned to his cave humming cheerfully.

The children breathed a sigh of relief and settled back to count the lakes.

That afternoon they pulled into a campsite north of

Huntsville and began to set up the tent with great enthusiasm. Father had packed the station wagon so that it would serve as a food storage room when the tent was removed. "Even the most determined raccoon has trouble raiding a closed car," he told the children.

When the tent was properly erected and the equipment readied for supper, the children rummaged through their suitcases and changed for swimming. Mom and Dad accompanied them to the lake. Paul had made certain that Uloc was released from the car before they left.

They planned to stay at this park at least two nights. "The hills are beautiful. I'll bet there's an impressive view of the lake from up there," Dad was saying. "We'll have to take a hike up the trails tomorrow, gang."

The children warmly greeted this plan, then raced into the water. The lake was cold.

When they returned to the campsite, they found no trace of Uloc.

"He's still around, though," whispered Doug. "His spear and cloak are under the car seat."

Supper was begun and finished, the dishes washed, and a fire lit. As the campers sat planning the next day's program, Dad glanced up into the darkness and exclaimed, "Look children, an owl up in that tree!"

Doug began to object, "That's not an owl, ..." when he recognized who it actually was.

It was good to know he was still around.

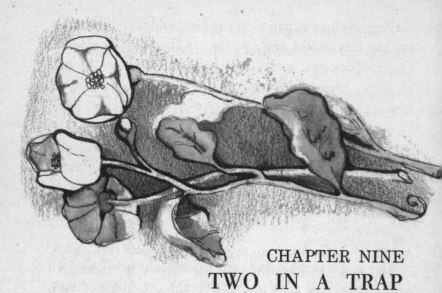

CHAPTER NINE
TWO IN A TRAP

E arly the following morning, the children sat watching the mist rise from the grey surface of the water as they waited for breakfast. The air was cool and the sun was only just beginning to overtop the ring of hills that cradled the lake.

"After we clean up, we'll go for that hike into the hills," Dad said. "Make sure you eat lots of breakfast, kids. You'll need all the energy you can muster."

As they washed their breakfast dishes, Ann whispered to Doug, "Is Uloc coming on the hike with us, or did he spend the whole night hooting in his tree?"

"Paul saw him early this morning. He seemed wide awake, Paul said. I don't think he ever really sleeps, you know."

After the final rituals of airing the bedding and whisking the bits of leaf and sand out of the tent, the group prepared for their safari into the hills. Doug took along an empty glass jar for any unusual insects they encountered. Paul checked Uloc's cornflakes box. It was empty and the cloak and spear were missing....

Amid great cries of self-encouragement, the exploration party set out, following a trail blazed by many others before them.

"As long as we stick to the trail, we'll be all right," Mom warned. "Don't go wandering off into the forest, you three."

The path wound through an old stand of pine and the forest floor was carpeted with a smooth layer of old needles. Only a few buttercups grew in isolated clusters along the path where the sun was able to break through the roof of boughs overhead. At several points, the family could see huge mossy-sided boulders, like motionless icebergs on a piney sea. Ann spotted a grosbeak in the lower branches while gathering a handful of the buttercups.

The trail pursued its well-worn course upwards to an area where vast, rocky outcroppings stood in layers, tiny cliffs running off along the hillside to vanish among the trees. The pine forest was giving way to stands of maple and groves of white birch.

No one spoke; only a bird broke the deep silence.

Once, when the children had gathered to examine a

group of toadstools sprouting from an ancient stump, they glimpsed a familiar fur-clad figure at the base of an immense basswood tree. When they looked again, Uloc had vanished.

"We'll beat you to the hilltop," called Dad from somewhere along the trail ahead. "Hurry up!"

"Coming!" answered Doug, only to find that Ann and Paul had wandered off to get a closer look at a rabbit that seemed strangely fascinating. He plunged into the forest to bring them back.

"Come on; we're not supposed to leave the trail."

Although he heard his companions scuffling their way through the dead pine leaves he received no answer.

Doug froze. For an instant he felt his sister was in terrible danger, although he could hear nothing. Panicking, he pushed his way through a thicket of birch seedlings and ran hard towards the place where he thought Ann and Paul should be. He stopped, mystified, in front of a large boulder that dominated the woodland. Apart from the thicket he had just passed, and this great stone, the forest floor was clear. He could see for hundreds of metres among the widely-spaced tree trunks, but there was no trace of Ann or of Paul.

Doug was about to search further when he spotted two things: at his feet was a scattered group of yellow blossoms, the buttercups Ann had been carrying. And on the rock itself, five grooves had been ripped through the mossy coating. His fingers and thumb fitted the ruts perfectly as he pulled his hand across the stone.

"What's going on?" wondered Doug. He was about to call his friends again when he heard a voice call his name.

"Doug! Get back from that rock, quickly! Come here! Now!" Uloc spoke with intense urgency. "Don't lean against the rock, Doug. There is a dreadful sense of Evil in this place!"

"What do you mean?" Doug's voice shook as he jumped back from the boulder. "What kind of evil?"

"The servants of Ga-Nakawasis were in this place last night. He has left his deadly palace in the Lost North, journeying south this far."

"But why?"

"By now, his spies have told him of my unguarded pool. He will try to trap me before I can find a new stream. He cannot touch me while I carry my stone, but I had forgotten my friends had no such shield. You have not the protection of the amulet unless I am with you. When you separated, I stayed with you. I am deeply sorry about the others."

A pain tightened in Doug's throat. "What are you saying?" he croaked. "Where are Ann and Paul?"

Uloc stared sadly at Doug's face. "Where are they?" He was screaming now, and Uloc flinched. "Answer me, Uloc!" Tears rolled down Doug's cheeks as he pleaded.

"Inside the rock, my friend. Ga-Nakawasis himself has taken them. The strange rabbit they were following

guided them to this place. It was one of his servants. Then Ga-Nakawasis seized them and they are now in his power."

"That's not true! It can't be," wailed Doug. But a glance at Uloc's face left no room for doubt. His breath continued in halting sobs.

"How can I get them out, Uloc? How can I reach them?"

"To reach them you need only walk through the rock; to get them out requires more."

"I'm going in after them," said Doug, brushing his eyes.

"Carry these, then," ordered Uloc, handing him the cloak and spear. "If the danger is too great, put on the cloak and return to me. This much safety I can offer you. The rock will not open for me if I carry the jade; without it we are all lost."

With the cloak and spear in one hand and his forgotten insect jar still clasped in the other, Doug leaned hard against the rock. To his astonishment, it opened like a curtain and he fell forward to his knees. He was inside the boulder!

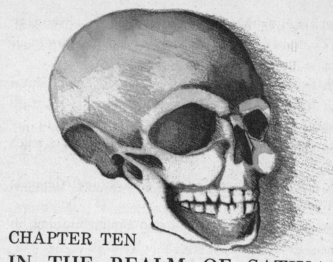

CHAPTER TEN
IN THE REALM OF SATIKA

At first Doug had trouble seeing anything at all in the terrible blackness of the boulder's interior, but gradually he could make out a faint patch of pale light, far ahead of him in the gloom. He edged nervously towards it.

All around him he could sense the closeness of the rock, as though he were walking through a very narrow passage. The floor seemed perfectly smooth and level, but the air was damp and musty-smelling. He was moving neither upwards nor downwards.

The patch of light was growing larger now. Soon he noticed that a dim glow marked the end of the passage. He moved more rapidly.

Presently, he stood in the doorway of a long narrow room with a very low ceiling; only half a metre above his head was the solid granite of the bedrock. The pale light seemed to filter in from everywhere; Doug could not see where it really came from.

He began to make his way carefully toward two large crimson objects at the far end of the strange hall. Coming closer, he recognized the faces of Paul and Ann amid the crimson. Throwing caution to the winds, he rushed toward them.

Both were seated on massive rocky thrones, brilliant red cloaks around their shoulders. Fine gold patterns ran through the folds of the robes which fell over their arms and knees to the floor. At their feet were all varieties of fruit and other delicacies. Gold circlets rimmed their foreheads; gold and silver lay heaped in nuggets on the floor. The wall behind them was studded with faintly glowing amethysts and other gems.

Doug gazed into the pale and expressionless faces of his sister and his chum. "What are you doing?" he asked.

Ann's voice sounded faintly through the shallow room. "We have been made rulers of a great land within the earth. You, too, can share our joy." (She didn't look or sound the least bit joyful to Doug.)

"You have only to bring the jadestone of Uloc to our Lord Satika."

"Where have I heard that name before?" Doug wondered.

While his sister spoke, Doug felt the spear of Uloc quivering in his hand. He knew from its vibration that she

spoke falsely. But why would she lie to him now?

"Come on, let's get out of here," he said, grabbing Ann's wrist. To his horror, as the red robes fell back, he saw that her hands and her feet were bound by leather strips to the throne on which she sat. Paul was tied as well.

A sudden, rasping, laugh behind him made Doug wheel around. Before him, stood a creature not much taller than himself, but veiled, hooded and draped in a white garment.

"You have no choice, fool," the figure croaked. "If you do not bring me the jadestone of Uloc, your companions will remain where they are until they starve. This is the realm of Satika, Lord of Hunger." The voice cackled an empty, horrifying, laugh. Doug felt as though a thousand worms were crawling over his body; he flipped the cloak onto his shoulder.

"Before I send you back to the sunlight," warned Satika, "listen to me well. Be sure to bring the stone. You cannot enter again without it, and the two rulers (he laughed again) cannot reach the food at their feet. I shall not kill them—you yourself will do so if you fail."

Losing all control, Doug hurled the insect jar at Satika. It struck hard, shattering the glass. The Lord of Hunger shuddered—then laughed. His veil fell back to reveal the hollow, nightmare, eyes of an empty skull!

"Uloc! Help me!" shrieked Doug, and suddenly found himself sitting on the forest floor beside Uloc.

"What did you learn?" asked the little man. But Doug was now unconscious, with an expression of absolute terror on his face.

Uloc succeeded in reviving him several minutes later. "It was terrible, Uloc," whispered Doug.

Uloc listened carefully without speaking.

"I saw a skull that talked. It said Ann and Paul would have to stay—chained up in there until they starve unless I bring Satika your amulet, Uloc. What do we do now? We can't let them starve to death under the ground."

"No, my friend, we cannot. I have asked too much of you already. There is only one thing left to do."

"What?"

"Exactly what Satika orders. He is the Lord of Hunger and will execute his threats without pity. To the hunting men, he was more fearsome than Ga-Nakawasis himself, for he did great and dreadful Evils. We must give him the jadestone so that he will free the others."

He took off the pouch which held the precious amulet and handed it to Doug.

"I shall follow you into the rock," Uloc continued. "If I am near the amulet there remains some hope of escape for us all. Without it, I perish."

Doug took the stone and walked into the boulder. He hesitated in the darkness until he felt Uloc stumble into his heel. Then he moved quietly along the passage to the pale glow at the far end.

Stepping into the grim light, he saw Ann and Paul still

bound to the thrones. Beside them, stood the gaunt figure of Satika.

"I have brought the stone," Doug said, the words rasping from his dry throat. "You must promise to free us all before I give it to you."

Satika's hollow voice almost froze Doug's senses. "When I have the jadestone in my hand, I will return you and your companions to the surface. I will not harm you, now or evermore."

Doug knew from the spear still in his hand that Satika was speaking the truth. He handed him the stone.

All three children immediately found themselves sitting on the path in the forest. A few seconds later, their parents reached them.

"Well, what a bunch of snails! Your mother and I went to the lookout and back, and here you are, resting, only halfway to the top. Youth is supposed to have more energy, not less . . . . .

"Here now, Doug, what are you crying about?"

CHAPTER ELEVEN
THE WALL BREAKS

"I guess we've been a little too rough on you children. After all, the amount of swimming you did yesterday must have drained an awful lot from you." The children's behaviour puzzled Mr. Torrance; Doug crying to himself, and Paul and Ann staring at the ground as though they had sunstroke. "Let's go get some lunch."

Doug stumbled down the trail to the campsite, but his mother had to lead Ann by the hand, and Paul, too, had to be guided.

"They're acting very strangely. Do you suppose they're sick—you know, too much sun, or some change in the food?" Mom was very worried.

After lunch, however, Ann and Paul were once more bouncing around the campsite, eagerly searching for ways to occupy the time until it was safe to plunge into the lake again. Only Doug continued to sit quietly at the picnic bench, absorbed in thought.

Ann was now loudly proclaiming her victory over Paul in a checker game. Doug noticed that she was even noisier and more active than usual.

After his second defeat, Paul strolled over to join Doug at the picnic table. Ann followed him. Relaxing on their camp cots, her parents were relieved by the sudden drop into silence.

"Hey, Doug, what's eating you? Don't you feel well?" Paul was becoming concerned.

"We've got to rescue him, Paul."

"Rescue who?" asked Ann.

"Uloc. We can't leave him there."

As he searched their confused faces, Doug realized that neither knew anything about Uloc's capture. Enquiring further, he learned they remembered nothing of their own imprisonment in the underground cavern. His voice dropped to a whisper as he related the morning's events to them. At times they seemed to disbelieve his tale, but enough hints of memory clouded their eyes to tell him they knew.

"When I think back, though, I don't really believe there was a skeleton under those clothes. Remember how Uloc said people saw him the way they expected to see him? I think it's like that with all the Old Order. When I heard Satika, I thought his laugh sounded spooky, like a ghost or something. So when I saw him, he looked just as scary as I thought he would. I'm not really afraid of him now, but he'll do something terrible to Uloc if we don't help."

"What can we do?" demanded Ann. "You said you couldn't walk back through the stone without Uloc's jade. How can we reach him?"

"I still have these," answered Doug, showing her the cloak and spear. "All I have to do is put it on and wish—and bingo! I'm with Uloc in that cavern. You two have to take Mom and Dad to the beach so they don't worry about my being gone. I'll stay here until you're all out of sight."

When the plan was decided upon, the conspirators broke up until it was time to go swimming. Doug announced that he would stay at the tent, his mother felt his forehead and declared he might be wise indeed to have a rest. She also threatened to stay and look after him, but all three children clamoured loudly that she had to go to the beach. In the face of all this urging, she got out her bathing suit and suntan lotion.

As soon as the others were safely down the path to the lake, Doug donned the cloak and wished himself to Uloc. His hands were shaking so badly that he very nearly dropped the spear.

Again his eyes took time to adjust to the gloom. As the darkness gradually became less intense around him, he recognized the seats on which Ann and Paul had been enthroned. Lying on one, with tight leather cords at his feet, chest, and neck, lashing his legs and arms painfully to the surface, was the small body of Uloc. The dark skin was pale, and the cord at his throat seemed to have cut off all breath, but the little man was still alive.

Doug fumbled at the cords, but his tugging only pulled the leather more tightly across Uloc's chest.

"Wish I had brought my knife," mumbled Doug, glancing about him helplessly. A glint of pale light on the floor caught his eye, and he raced across to get a piece of the broken insect jar.

Uloc was soon freed, but Doug had to carry the now unconscious body like a worn-out teddy bear. He was not certain Uloc could live much longer.

"Now, where's the exit?" he wondered, staggering to a dark recess in the wall.

The passageway was only a little more than a metre deep, leading nowhere. Doug's heart sank, but he found something of great importance; something that his eagerness to rescue Uloc had erased from his mind. There, on a narrow ledge in the rock, was the pouch containing the jade. As he placed the stone around Uloc's neck, the little man opened his eyes in amazement.

"What are you doing here, Doug? Satika will capture you also! Get out before it is too late for you."

An icy voice riveted Doug's attention. "You had your freedom, but returned here. Now I shall soon destroy you as I have destroyed millions of other men."

In his hand, Doug felt Uloc's spear vibrate as Satika spoke. He forced his courage.

"You're bluffing, Satika. I don't think you can do anything to me. And Uloc has his stone again—you can't harm him either."

"So, Boy, you know that much of the Old Order? In a child of mankind such understanding is rare. Very well, you are right, at least for the time being. But consider this.

"I promised never to harm you or your two friends. I made no such pledge for Uloc's safety. Once he has left his jadestone here, I shall bring the end upon him. And he cannot pass through the wall without setting aside the amulet. As the jade is his protection, so the rock shields me from intruders. Uloc's guardian cannot penetrate mine while he carries it.

"Consider also, that although I gave my word not to harm you, you may not leave this hall without my permission. You slipped in through my wall once, I know not how. It will not be so again."

Satika's voice slowed, and the menace in his tone crackled in Doug's ears.

"Therefore, man child, you and Uloc may stay here in this cavern, to watch each other, to despair of ever again seeing the sun. Uloc may not pass through the wall with his jade, and you may not pass at all.

Satika's laughter echoed through the room; his shape slipped away as if it were mist rising from a lake.

72

"What do we do now, Uloc?" Doug was already beginning to feel a warm wetness in his eyes.

"Hush, my friend," warned Uloc. "Come to the entry, where you first came in this morning. The answer is simple, because Satika, for all his blind pride, does not understand the powers of Uloc's cloak and spear."

Doug felt his way cautiously along the narrow passageway to the rock surface. In the intense blackness, he rammed his forehead against the wall that blocked their exit to the sunlight. His skull throbbed with pain.

Uloc clambered up Doug's leg and arm to his shoulder and whispered carefully into his ear.

"Now, listen, for if we hesitate for even a few seconds, we lose all. I will release the jade into your hand and walk through the entry-stone. As soon as I go, use the cloak. Do you understand?" whispered Uloc.

"Yes." His head ached so much that Doug nearly lost his balance.

Uloc lowered himself to the floor and signalled Doug to take the jade. In the underground night Doug could not see if his friend had gone, but he waited only a split instant before clutching the cloak to his shoulder. He felt dizzy.

The cloak slid to the floor before Doug could wish himself away, and he spent several agonized seconds groping around the ground. As he searched he caught sight of a white form moving toward him from nowhere, and heard a wild shriek of fury. He snatched up the cloak

again and thought the wish. An icy pain pierced his shoulder.

Instantly he was standing on the soft brown forest duff outside, blinking at the bright sparkles of light filtering among the leaves. The pain in his head and arm vanished.

"You have done well, my friend," said Uloc, clasping the pouch.

"Is it over, Uloc? Are we safe?"

"You have the pledge of Satika himself, and I have the jade again. Yes, Doug. We are all safe."

Doug ran back to the trail, with Uloc at his heels. He hurried down, past the campsite, past the main roadway, on through the pines to the beach.

"It's over, it's all right," he cried happily to the others.

Paul and Ann cheered from the water.

"I'm glad you're better, dear," exclaimed his mother. "I was just coming up to see you again."

Doug stood on the sand grinning.

CHAPTER TWELVE
THE END,
THE BEGINNING

For the next eight days, they spent a leisurely vacation surrounded by the woods, the rocks, the lakes, of Northern Ontario. They saw the huge tracts of parkland and forest preserves, and the mines at Kirkland Lake; they even reached Timmins.

One outcome of the adventure was the freedom the children gained in the water. They swam better than they had ever dreamed of swimming, and even Dad remarked that they behaved like seals.

A less pleasant result was a white mark on Doug's shoulder. Paul noticed it first, saying it looked almost like a handprint, but the fingers were too long and thin. The mark disappeared gradually after a few days.

Through the whole journey Uloc was there, stretched

out in his cornflake cave while the car sped along the highway, or watching from some secret vantage point as the campers sat gathered around the fire on crisp northern evenings. He was as ever-present as the mosquitoes that clouded the sky, but far more comforting.

Even as they began their return trip, Uloc was with them. The children were puzzled by his continued presence, and one evening Doug braved the insects and walked a little way into the forest.

"Uloc, are you there?"

"Yes."

"I want to ask a question."

The stocky little figure stood before him unexpectedly.

"Have you found your new stream?" asked Doug.

"Yes, I have, my friend."

"Where is it? Why don't you go to it?"

"But I am going to it. It flows through a town far from here, close to an iron trail, fed by a smoking house."

"Hey, that sounds like .... I mean, is it ..?"

"Yes, I am returning to my old pool, weary and corrupt though it be. If children of the New Order can endure so much evil, then the Old Order, too, must prove itself anew. You have showed me that men may be wise and brave as well as lazy and foolish. And I myself have been foolish, running away from my old stream. I must continue my task; I will cleanse and purify its waters. I truly know now what the saying means, 'From the oldest comes the new.'"

"Maybe we can help," suggested Doug. "We can gather up the old cans and bottles and tires. Maybe Paul's father would change the factory sewer—I'm sure he would. If enough people wanted, the field and The Bush could be made into a park."

But Uloc had melted again into the night.

"Darn these mosquitoes," muttered Doug, and scrambled back to whisper the good news.